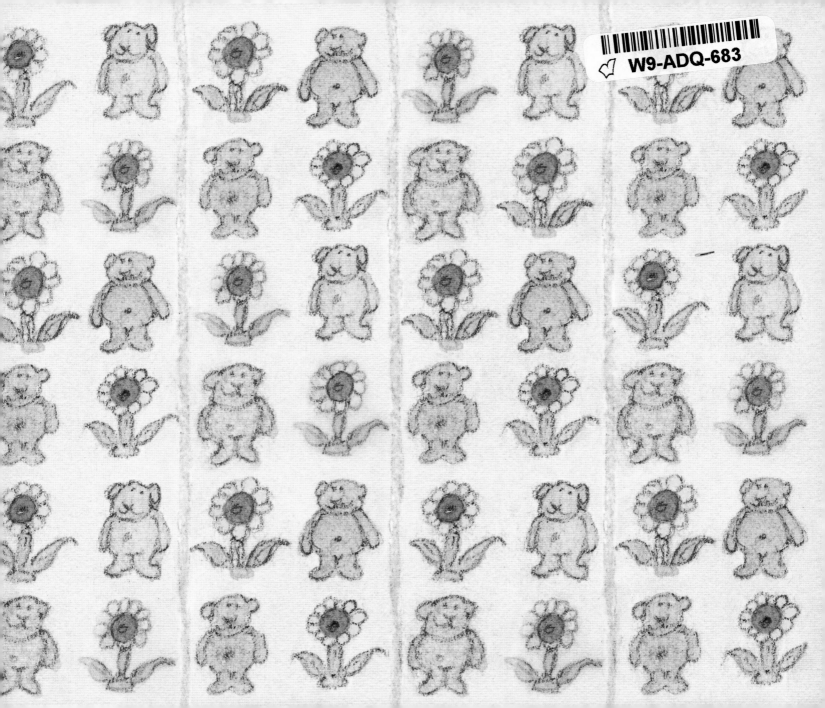

story by Ruth Krauss
pictures by Maurice Sendak

Washing hairs

every

wheres

First published in hardback in Great Britain by HarperCollins Children's Books in 2005

1 3 5 7 9 10 8 6 4 2

ISBN: 0-00-720662-3

Text copyright © Ruth Krauss 1948

Copyright renewed 1976 by Ruth Krauss

Pictures copyright © Maurice Sendak 2005

Hand lettering by Tom Starace

Ruth Krauss's text for BEARS, *with pictures by Phyllis Rowand, was first published in 1948 by Harper & Brothers*

www.harpercollinschildrensbooks.co.uk

Michael di Capua Books · HarperCollins Publishers